CUENTO DE LUZ

*To the Tree House that gave me
so many wonderful moments during my childhood.*

- María Quintana Silva -

*When the trees burst into flower, they light up the forest.
Then we are lit up with them.*

- Silvia Álvarez -

Waterproof and tear resistant
Produced without water, without trees and without bleach
Saves 50% of energy compared to normal paper

The Last Tree
Text © 2018 María Quintana Silva
Illustrations © 2018 Silvia Álvarez
This edition © 2018 Cuento de Luz SL
Calle Claveles, 10 | Urb. Monteclaro | Pozuelo de Alarcón | 28223 | Madrid | Spain
www.cuentodeluz.com
Title in Spanish: *El último árbol*
English translation by Jon Brokenbrow
First printing
Printed in PRC by Shanghai Chenxi Printing Co., Ltd. September 2018, print number 1651-7
ISBN: 978-84-16733-46-0

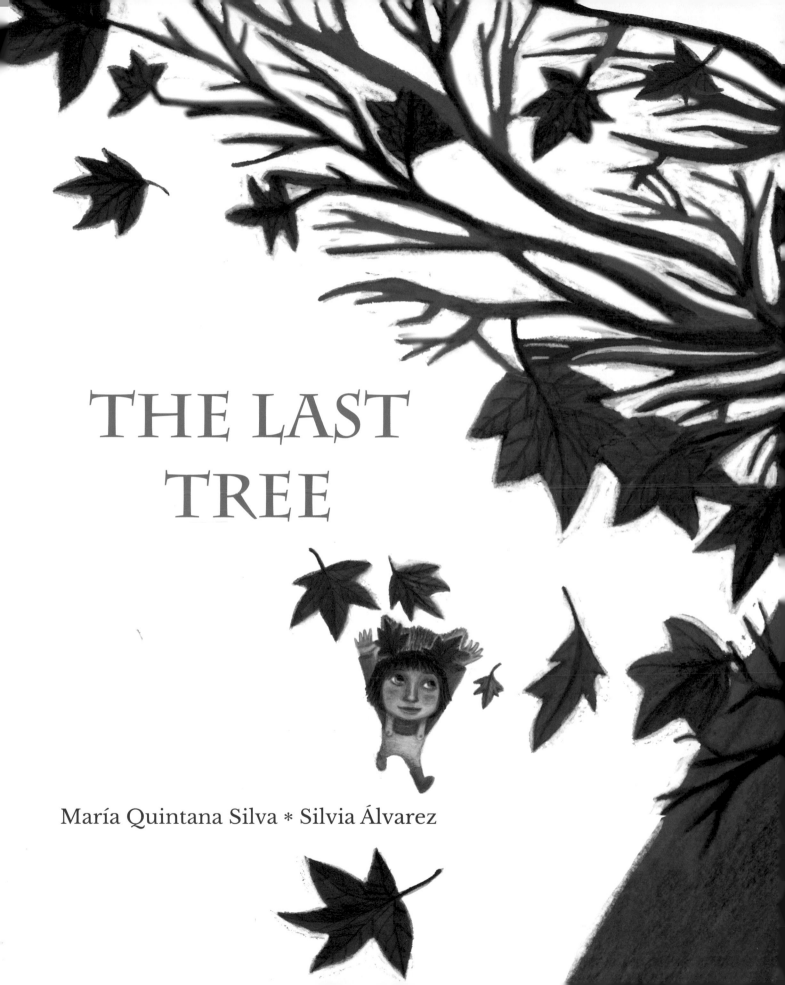

THE LAST TREE

María Quintana Silva * Silvia Álvarez

One night, the trees decided it was time to leave. They yanked out their roots, and dragged themselves off across the fields.

The next morning, Goran set off towards school. It was too hot, and there was no shade to protect him.

When he arrived, he realized what had happened: the forest had disappeared, and only holes remained in the ground where the trees had once stood.

"What happened?" Goran asked the animals who were also looking at the barren landscape.

"The trees have gone!" said an old squirrel.

"And where are those birds going?" asked the lynx, seeing a family of hummingbirds buzzing through the sky with bags in their claws.

"We're moving to another nest; one that doesn't move around so much!" yelled Father Hummingbird.

"We'll all have to find new homes," added the squirrel, and one by one, the animals set off to find them.

At school, Goran wondered if the tree in his garden had also disappeared. In the springtime, he loved to swing from its branches.

In the summer, its leafy shade protected him from the hot sun.

In the autumn, he loved to play with the beautifully colored leaves that fell to the ground.

In the cold winter, Goran would see the tree from his window, and it would greet him by shaking its branches.

It was the guardian of the garden. It was his friend.

When school was over, Goran hurried to leave. A thick, grey smog filled the city streets. It was hot, and it was difficult to breathe.

When he arrived home, his tree was still there, but not for long: it was already pulling up its roots.

"Don't do it!" cried Goran, as his throat began to sting more and more. "You're the last tree!"

"Precisely! I'd better be going!" said the tree, making sure that all of its leaves were ready to leave.

"But we can't survive without trees . . . aren't you happy here?" asked Goran, as he began to cough loudly.

"I prefer to leave by my own roots, before I get burnt to ash, or cut into a thousand pieces," replied the tree. The earth shook as it headed off into the choking mist.

Goran cleared his throat, and yelled: "Wait!
You're forgetting something!"

The tree had already reached the middle of the garden,
and turned around.

"I'm keeping the birdhouse," it said. "My friends
the birds need it."

"It's not the birdhouse. It's just that . . .
winter's coming, and where will you go in
all this cold?" asked Goran, attempting
to make the tree stay behind.

The tree stopped, and thought awhile.
"You're right. I don't think I'll get too far with these old roots."

"Then stay here! Rest, and have a nap." Said Goran. "When you wake up, I'm sure you'll find a good reason to stay. If you don't, you can go, and I won't argue again."

The tree nodded. "But I'm warning you, I'm looking for somewhere nice and quiet to spend the next hundred years," it said, looking at the landscape around it. Then it turned around, trundled back to its spot, and fell asleep.

Throughout the whole winter, Goran and his friends worked hard to replant the forest with all kinds of trees.

Little by little, the grey smog disappeared. The townspeople stopped coughing, and could walk without feeling faint. The birds returned to their nests high in the canopies, and the squirrels leapt from branch to branch.

Then they made a final effort: they picked up all of the leftover, thrown away, or unused paper they could find, and they recycled it.

Spring arrived, and the last tree woke up.
All around it, trees of different sizes and
colors were keeping it company.

Its branches were bursting with life. Goran hugged its trunk as hard as he could.

"You see?" said Goran. "I promise this will be a perfect place for you, for the next hundred years, and more!"

That morning, the last tree decided it was worth staying behind.

No trees were harmed in making this story.

OCT 3 1 2019